The Secret Fairy in
Fairyland

To JD with love
Penny Dann

To Mum, my best friend
Claire Freedman

First published in Great Britain in 2001 by
ORCHARD BOOKS
96 Leonard Street, London EC2A 4XD
Orchard Books Australia
Unit 31/56 O'Riordan Street, Alexandria, NSW 2015
ISBN 1 84121 723 9
Illustrations © Penny Dann 2001
Text © Claire Freedman 2001
The right of Penny Dann to be identified as the illustrator
and Claire Freedman as the author of this book has been
asserted by them in accordance with the Copyright,
Designs and Patents Act, 1988.
A CIP catalogue record for this book is available from
the British Library.
10 9 8 7 6 5 4 3
Printed in Singapore

The Secret Fairy in Fairyland

Welcome to my world!

As told by the Fairies to
Penny Dann and Claire Freedman

ORCHARD BOOKS

✴ Contents ✴

Welcome to Fairyland

Hi, Secret Fairy fans! Come and visit Fairyland and meet all my best fairy friends. It's great fun here – there are always lots of parties to go to and fairy work to be done. Fairyland is a very busy place!

I'm Nettle. I'm Blossom's special best friend. She says I'm great fun to be with because I get up to all kinds of mischief. Ooops!

Hello! I'm Bluebell and at my hair and beauty parlour Blossom and all the fairies share their secrets with me!

Buzz!

✶ Blossom and the Missing Necklace ✶

One day in spring, Blossom was out walking when she came across a fairy flower trail.

Who has left this?

I wonder who's in there. Hello?

Excitedly, Blossom followed the trail. It led to a secret door in the palace.

I really need your help.

DANCING COMPETITION
* * *
the best dancer will be awarded the Fairy Queen's SURPRISE PRIZE!

I'll do my best, Your Majesty.

Inside, Blossom found the Fairy Queen. She seemed upset and explained that she had lost a special necklace, which was to be won at the Fairy Dancing Competition that afternoon.

Blossom agreed to help. She would make a
new necklace so no one would know.

Good luck,
Blossom. And
thank you.

Don't worry.
Your secret is safe –
I won't even tell
Nettle.

I must find
something even
prettier.

Back at her boutique, Blossom searched
her fairy jewels. None looked quite right.

Here you are,
Blossom.

One of
every colour!

We're
always happy
to help!

It's perfect,
thank you!

Blossom decided to visit the tree tops. The birds gave her some feathers
and the friendly ladybirds helped string the feathers together.

This should
do the trick!

…A
masterpiece!

Yoo-hoo!
Blossom!

We've
come to call
for you!

Oh no!
They mustn't see
the necklace!

At the boutique, Blossom sprinkled the
necklace with fairy dust. Now it really glittered!

Blossom had forgotten that Nettle and Bluebell were picking her up on their way to the dance.

Nettle and Bluebell couldn't understand why Blossom wasn't ready to go.

After her friends had left, Blossom tidied up a little then put on her party dress.

It wasn't until she was leaving for the dancing competition that Blossom remembered the necklace. But where had she put it? She searched everywhere…

Blossom rushed to the palace as fast as she could, to explain to the Queen that she had lost the second necklace!

Blossom quickly took the necklace off and handed it to the Queen.

Blossom relaxed and really enjoyed the dancing. But both Blossom and the Queen laughed out loud when the winner was announced! And of course, Blossom pretended to be surprised when the Fairy Queen handed her the prize necklace!

✶ Fairyland Jewellery ✶

Glitterbug Feather Necklace

You will need: Three feathers
Thin coloured card ✶ A penny
Pencil ✶ Scissors ✶ Clear glue
A length of cord long enough to fit over your head ✶ Fairyland stickers

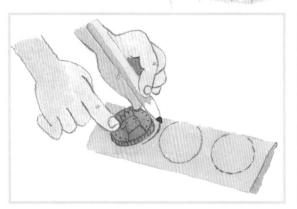

1. Fold the card in half. Place the penny so that it hangs over the fold and draw around it. Do this 3 times. Cut these card beads out but don't cut through the folded spines.

2. Find the middle of your length of cord, and hang a card bead over it. Apply glue to the inside of the bead and press the sticky sides together to hold in place on the cord.

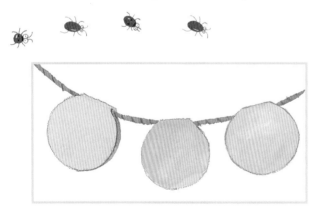

3. Hang two beads, evenly spaced, on either side of the centre bead. Glue them onto the cord in the same way and allow to dry.

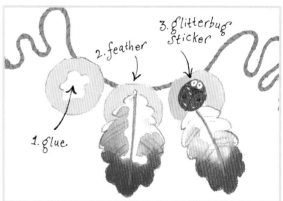

4. Glue a feather on top of each bead so that they hang down. Allow to dry and add glitterbug stickers to each feather, as shown.

Glitterbug Feather Brooch

Now cut out a single circle shape
from card using a 10 pence coin.
Decorate it in the same way.
Attach a safety pin to the back of
the brooch with a small piece
of sticky tape – mind your fingers!

Sparkle Rings and Spangly Bangles

For the rings:

1. Cut a piece of card about 1cm by 6cm. Overlap the edges and
glue together to make a ring that will fit on your finger.

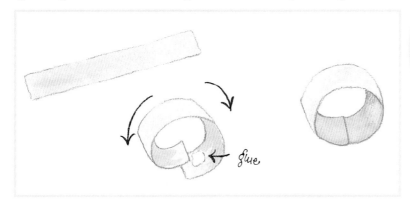

glue

2. Allow to dry before
sticking sparkling Fairyland
stickers all around the ring.

For the bangles:

1. Cut a piece of
card about 4cm
by 20cm. Cut a
wiggly shape
along both
edges. Overlap
the ends and
glue to make a
bangle that fits
over your hand.

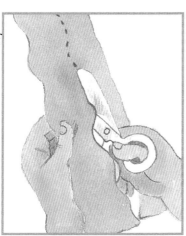

2. Decorate with beautiful spangly stickers.

Fairy Fashion Parade

Spring and Summer Surprises

My friend Rosebud and the fashion fairies sew flower petals together to make fairy dresses. Rosebud has invited us all to the Summer Fairy Fashion Parade.

It looks like the fashion fairies have thought of everything for summer! Don't you love those stripy beach towels made from green moss and marigold petals? Take a look at the starfish flip-flops too! Now all the fairies can sunbathe on the beach in style! Hurry up, holiday time!

✳ The Clumsy Fairy ✳

It was almost time for Fairyland's May Ball. All the
fairies were excitedly discussing what to wear.

"I wonder who will be crowned May
Princess this year," Blossom said.

"Well, it won't be me!" joked
Hollyhock. "I'm so clumsy I'd
probably drop the crown and break it!"

The other fairies all had a fit of the
giggles at this. It was true – Hollyhock
was a very clumsy and messy fairy. But she
was so friendly and funny that it didn't
matter a bit and everyone loved her.

On the morning of the ball, Hollyhock was flying
in the woods. She was looking for some petals to make into a necklace but
some pretty flowers caught her eye. Hollyhock flew down to look at them.

But she didn't notice an old tree stump and
crashed straight into it!

"Clumsy me!" she cried. "Now
I've got moss stains on my skirt and
I've squashed the primroses!"

As Hollyhock dusted herself
down she saw something glinting
amongst the leaves below. She flew
down and picked it up. It was a
lovely sparkly brooch.

"This belongs to Rosebud, the fashion fairy," Hollyhock gasped. "It's been missing for ages. Oh, she will be pleased I've found it."

Hollyhock rushed over to see Rosebud at once. She found her busily adding the final touches to the Fairy Queen's beautiful ball gown. Rosebud was delighted to have her brooch back.

"Well done for finding it," she told Hollyhock. "Now I can wear it to the ball tonight. Is there anything I can do to thank you?" she asked.

Hollyhock hesitated.

"I wonder, could you make *me* look wonderful for the ball?" she asked hopefully. "However hard I try, I always end up looking a silly mess!"

"No problem!" Rosebud replied. "I'm not Fairyland's top fashion fairy for nothing. We'll get to work at once!"

What an afternoon Hollyhock had! While one fairy styled her hair, others worked on her make-up and dress. At long last she was ready for the ball.

"Oooh!" Hollyhock gasped in amazement as she stared at her reflection in the mirror, "I don't look like me any more. I look like a… princess!"

"It's a lovely dress," Rosebud said. "Pink and purple with lilac shoes and a bag to match."

"My face looks so different too," Hollyhock said with delight.

"It's the rainbow make-up," Rosebud replied. "Wait, you need one final touch!" and she sprayed Hollyhock with the most gorgeous perfume.

Hollyhock arrived at the ball wondering what her friends might say when they saw her.

"They probably won't even recognise me," she thought. And no one did!

"Hello, Blossom! Hi, Bluebell!" Hollyhock called. "Surprise – it's me!" But the music was so loud they couldn't hear her and just wondered who she was.

Feeling disappointed, Hollyhock decided to find something to eat. The food looked delicious and she was just about to take a huge bite of strawberry cake, when she had a worrying thought.

"Knowing me, I'll spill food all down my dress and spoil it," she sighed. She put down the cake and headed for the dance floor instead. It was crowded with fairies whirling and swirling about. Hollyhock longed to join in but she knew what would happen if she did. She'd trip over someone's feet and end up breaking a shoe. So Hollyhock sat in a corner feeling glum, watching the other fairies enjoy themselves. Suddenly she made a decision.

She rushed home, changed into her red
dress and washed off some of the make-up!

"Now I look and feel like me again,"
she said. "And I can have some fun!"

In no time Hollyhock was back at the ball.

"At last – you're here!" called Blossom.

"We missed you!" Bluebell said. "Never
mind, you're just in time to hear who has
been chosen as the May Princess."

Everyone hushed as the Fairy Queen announced the winner – Hollyhock!

"Me?" gasped Hollyhock, knocking over a table as she rushed to receive her
crown from the Fairy Queen. "But I'm such a hopelessly clumsy fairy."

"And a very nice one too," the Fairy Queen said as everyone clapped.
Happily, Hollyhock helped herself to some strawberry cake. And when she
accidentally bumped into another fairy and sent the crown flying into the jelly,
even the Fairy Queen laughed!

✶ Ballet with Blossom ✶

Welcome to your first fairy ballet class. Hollyhock and Blossom are going to show you some basic ballet steps.

Bluebell is playing the music for us on the piano. Music, Maestro!

1. Begin with your legs and feet turned out. Stand with both heels together and turn out your legs so that your toes point outwards. This is called *first position*.

This is not right!

2. Now place your feet apart, like this. Keep your feet and toes turned right out. This is called *second position*.

Tut, tut!

BUMP!

3. Next, cross the heel of one foot halfway in front of the middle of the other foot. Remember to stand up straight and keep your feet turned outwards. This is *third position*.

It helps to wear clothes you can move easily in, like a leotard or leggings. Wear soft shoes or go barefoot. Tie your hair up too.

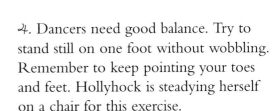

4. Dancers need good balance. Try to stand still on one foot without wobbling. Remember to keep pointing your toes and feet. Hollyhock is steadying herself on a chair for this exercise.

Mmm...

Oops, I nearly did the splits!

5. Now try this well-known position called an *arabesque*. Balance on one leg with your other leg stretched out behind you. Hold your arms out gracefully.

Careful, Hollyhock! I think your shoes have come undone.

Whoa! I don't feel so well!

6. Make up a dance using all these different positions. Finish with a twirl, called a *pirouette*. Spin around as fast as you can. Well done. Take a bow!

I did tell her!

✦ Fairyland Friends ✦

Introduced by Lavender and her insect friends

> We share our lives with our animal neighbours. They help us with the day-to-day running of Fairyland.

> Let us all count together. One leg, two legs...

The centipedes and millipedes help out at Fairyland School. They're very handy for teaching the little fairies how to count.

The Fairy Queen's bees are busy all summer long. They collect sweet nectar from the flowers to make into delicious honey.

The fashion fairies follow the bees wherever they go! That's how they know where to find the prettiest petals for their fairy dresses.

> Cake crumbs!

The ants keep Fairyland clean and tidy. Every evening they gather up the crumbs from parties and picnics. The goodies are marched back to the ants' nest for supper!

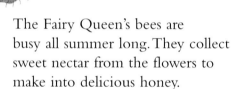

The ladybirds and caterpillars string dewdrops and berries onto blades of grass, to make necklaces and dangly earrings for Blossom's Boutique.

Blossom's Boutique

It's beautiful!

For you!

The Chirping Crickets are a favourite bug band. All the fairies enjoy listening to the wonderful music they make!

Spiders are useful too. They catch tiny dewdrops in their webs. Then the raindrop fairies collect the delicate dewdrops in acorn cups.

Take your partners for the butterfly waltz.

Dance School

Everyone in Fairyland loves to dance. So the butterflies run their famous Flutterby Dance School. Lessons are held every day in the Fairy Queen's palace ballroom.

⋆ Are You Animal Friendly? ⋆

Do you love animals?
Would you know what to do in a
creature crisis? Try my quiz to find out how
animal friendly you really are. On a piece
of paper, write down each answer you
would choose.

1. You're watering the Fairyland vegetable garden when
you spot a new rabbit hole close by. Do you:
A) Get cross! Those rabbits will munch through
your vegetables in no time!
B) Feel pleased – and hope to spot some
baby bunnies.
C) Leave a few carrots out for the rabbits to eat.

Yap!

2. You'd love a little puppy, but you work in the
perfume factory all day, and there's no one at
home to look after it. Would you:
A) Get a puppy anyway – and leave him
alone all day.
B) Have fun walking your neighbour's
little dog each evening.
C) Settle for a goldfish.

3. The Fairy Queen asks you to look after
the hedgehogs living at the bottom of
the palace gardens. Do you:
A) Give the hedgehogs some leftovers
from your tea.
B) Leave them water and a plate of dog food.
C) Leave out some bread and milk.

4. Whilst walking in Fairyland woods, you spot two blackbirds building their nest. Would you:

A) Take the nest home with you to show your friends.

B) Watch quietly from a distance – you don't want to disturb the birds.

C) Climb the tree for a better look.

Oooh, what a beautiful starfish!

5. You're on holiday at the seaside, and find a beautiful starfish in a rock pool. What do you do?

A) Take it home – it would look great in your aquarium.

B) Admire the starfish – but don't touch it.

C) Carry it inside and try and feed it.

How did you score?

Mostly A

Sometimes you seem to forget that animals have feelings too! Try reading up more about their needs, and you'll soon be creature kind.

Mostly B

You are a real animal lover. You know exactly how to care for creatures big and small. Keep it up and you'll be every animal's friend.

Mostly C

You like animals and try hard to help them. You still have a little more to learn about caring for them, but you're on the right track!

Strawberry Ladybirds

You will need:
Large strawberries
A bar of chocolate
Greaseproof paper
A small clean paintbrush
One large and one small heatproof bowl

1. Carefully remove the stalks from the strawberries. Cut them in half and lay flat-side-down on a sheet of greaseproof paper.

2. Break the chocolate into a small bowl. Place the small bowl inside the larger bowl and ask an adult to pour boiling water in between the two, halfway up the side. Leave for five minutes then carefully remove the small bowl. Stir the chocolate with a spoon.

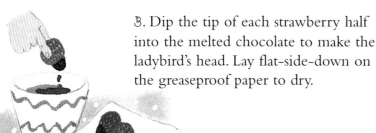

3. Dip the tip of each strawberry half into the melted chocolate to make the ladybird's head. Lay flat-side-down on the greaseproof paper to dry.

4. Use the brush to paint on a chocolate wing-case and spots. Allow the chocolate to set.

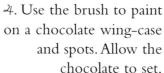

Hello...?

Blossom's Tip
Try making chocolate rose leaves. Dip the shiny side of clean rose leaves into the melted chocolate. Leave to harden and peel off!

More tea, Violet?

5. Arrange the ladybirds and leaves on a pretty plate and share with friends!

✳ Blossom's Seashore Surprise ✳

Blossom and her friends have been having a great
seaside holiday. But the week is nearly over.

Let's hold a farewell beach party!

I don't want to go home.

The next day, the fairies began
to get everything ready
for their beach party.

I'm decorating the party area with flowers.

I'll prepare the food.

What else will we need?

Why not organise the entertainment?

Everyone was busy, except for Blossom.
For once, she couldn't think how to help.

Blossom walked
along the beach,
trying to plan
some party games.
Suddenly, she
heard the most
beautiful singing!

Who's that singing?

To Blossom's surprise it was a mermaid! She smiled at Blossom and said that her name was Coral.

What a lovely voice you have.

Thank you, I love to sing – I do it all the time!

When Coral heard about the fairies' party, she had an idea for the entertainment.

I'd like to sing for you all at the party.

Gosh, would you?

What fun this will be!

Tee-hee! I'll hide here until you call my name!

Blossom and Coral arrived back at the beach as the party was about to begin.

A mermaid!

Hurrah!

Clever Blossom!

Sing us another song, Coral!

Three cheers for Coral!

As soon as everyone had eaten, Blossom sat them down and called to Coral. The other fairies could hardly believe it and they loved Coral's singing!

⋆ Perfect Party Tiara ⋆

Make my Secret Fairy tiara and crown yourself Sea Queen!

You will need:

A tape measure ⋆ A large silver or gold cake doily about 20cm across
Thin silver or gold card ⋆ Clear glue ⋆ Scissors ⋆ Fairyland stickers

1. First make the headband. Measure around your head and add on 4cm. Cut out a strip of coloured card 3cm wide to the length of your head measurement. Overlap the ends by 4cm and glue the ends of the card together to make the base of your tiara. Leave to dry.

2. Make a fold across the doily about 8cm deep. Cut across the fold.

3. Apply glue along the back of the piece of doily and attach it to the front of the headband.

4. Find the spangly seashells among the Fairyland stickers and stick them all over the tiara, to decorate it.

⋆ Hair and Beauty Secrets ⋆

From Bluebell's Beauty Parlour

Wheee!

Bluebell is a very talented hairstylist. Fairies come from far and wide to have their hair done here. I've asked Bluebell to show you how to make some of her beautiful hair creations. Hollyhock, Nettle and I are going to be Bluebell's models – what fun!

It is best to find a friend and style each other's hair. Before you start styling you should brush your hair smoothly. You will need a comb to begin each style and a mirror to see the end results!

We've used ribbons in two different colours.

Beauty Bows
modelled by Nettle

You will need:
4 lengths of narrow ribbon
(each 26cm long) ⋆ 4 hairgrips

1. Tie a knot in the middle of each piece of ribbon.
2. Slide a hairgrip through the back of each knot.
3. Tie a bow on top of each knot.
4. Brush your hair and use the comb to make a centre parting.
5. Put two bow grips on each side of your hair, just above your ears.

This hairstyle is easy to do!

This looks great on long hair.

Ribbon Twists
modelled by Hollyhock
You will need:
2 pieces of narrow ribbon
(twice the length of your hair),
4 small, matching hairbands

1. Take the comb and make a middle parting down the back of your head. Gather each side into a bunch and secure at the top and bottom with the hairbands.
2. Loop a ribbon through one of the top bands. Pull it to make equal lengths both sides.
3. Twist the ribbons round and round the bunch, crossing the ribbons over each other as you go. Knot the ribbon ends into a bow at the bottom hairband.

Bunches of Fun
modelled by Blossom
You will need:
4 small covered hairbands * 4 ribbons

1. Divide your hair into a middle parting again with the comb.
2. Keep one half out of the way with a band.
3. With your comb draw another parting across the centre of the loose hair. Secure each section with a band.
4. Tie bows over these two hairbands with ribbons.
5. Repeat on hair on the other side of your head.

Wear your special Fairyland nail tattoo stickers, to add the finishing touch!

This is such a cute hairstyle!

Fizzy Fairy Pop

Bluebell serves these refreshing drinks in her beauty parlour. I like sipping them while I'm having my hair done! Each recipe serves four fairies.

Fizzy Fairy Floats

You will need: A bottle of cherryade ✶ Vanilla ice cream
Hundreds and thousands or pink sugar strands ✶ Glasses ✶ Straws

1. Fill each glass three-quarters full of cherryade.

2. Add a scoop of vanilla ice cream to each glass.

3. Sprinkle lots of hundreds and thousands or sugar strands over the ice cream.

Droool! I'm feeling rather thirsty, Bluebell.

4. Top with a straw and serve at once.

Long Green Fairy Fizz

You will need: A bottle of lemonade ⋆ Lime juice cordial
Green food colouring ⋆ 2 kiwi fruits ⋆ Glasses ⋆ Straws

1. Peel and slice the kiwi fruits. Put a few slices into each glass.

2. Pour a little lime juice cordial and a drop of the food colouring into each glass.

3. Fill the glasses up with lemonade. Add a straw to each then serve and slurp!

Party Umbrella

You will need: Pretty paper cake cases
Blu-Tack™⋆ Cocktail sticks ⋆ Sticky tape ⋆ Scissors

Bluebell tops her fairy fizz drinks with a pretty umbrella.

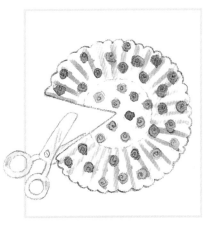 

1. Gently flatten a cake case a little with your palm and cut a triangle out of the circle of paper, as shown.

2. Overlap the cut edges and tape them together, putting tape on both sides of the paper umbrella.

3. Push a cocktail stick through the centre of the umbrella and out the other side, into a ball of Blu-Tack.™

Look under your birthday month to discover your secret fairy jewel sign.

⋆ Fairy Horoscopes ⋆

Written by Mystic Moth

January Fairy Jewel – Sapphire

Sapphire fairies are confident and love adventure. They make great leaders (the Fairy Queen is a Sapphire). Sapphire fairies like to keep busy all day long – but they must try not to rush into things too quickly.

February Fairy Jewel – Opal

Opal fairies make very good and loyal friends. They love pretty things and dressing up in beautiful clothes. Opal fairies are also good at sharing with other fairies. They can be a bit scared of taking risks at times.

March Fairy Jewel – Amethyst

Amethyst fairies are very easy-going and are fun to be with. They feel happiest out of doors, in the countryside. Amethyst fairies can be terrible time-keepers and often arrive late at parties but make up for it once they arrive.

April Fairy Jewel – Emerald

Emerald fairies are home-loving and often make wonderful cooks. They prefer to spend a quiet night in, rather than going to a noisy party. Emerald fairies like to have one special close friend (usually another Emerald fairy!).

May Fairy Jewel – Jade

Jade fairies always look neat and love tidying things up! They are dainty and graceful, and are often good at dancing. Jade fairies can sometimes be a little bit shy at meeting new people – but are always liked by everyone.

June Fairy Jewel – Turquoise

Parties are Turquoise fairies' favourite times. They are often good singers or actors and enjoy performing for their friends. Turquoise fairies like to be in the centre of a crowd and are great at organising events. They must try not to be too bossy.

July Fairy Jewel – Ruby

Ruby fairies are full of fun! They are always giggling with friends and telling silly jokes. They are also good at explaining ideas to other fairies. Ruby fairies only have one fault – they are non-stop chatterboxes!

August Fairy Jewel – Coral

Coral fairies are adventurous. They enjoy climbing trees, cycling on their bikes and exploring exciting new places. Coral fairies love animals of every kind and tend to keep lots of pets. They can be rather messy fairies and hate clearing up!

September Fairy Jewel – Amber

Amber fairies are very artistic. They like to paint and are clever at sewing and making their own clothes. Because they are such good listeners, they have plenty of friends. But don't ask one for advice – Amber fairies can never make their minds up about anything!

October Fairy Jewel – Topaz

Topaz fairies are sporty types. They are enthusiastic about everything they do and are full of good ideas. When they're not playing games, Topaz fairies often have their nose in a good book. Topaz fairies must try and remember to share more with their friends.

November Fairy Jewel – Moonstone

Moonstone fairies are always happy and cheerful. They are big nature lovers. If they find an injured animal you can bet that they'll want to care for it. They never forget to leave food out for the birds in winter. Moonstone fairies must remember to look after themselves too!

December Fairy Jewel – Diamond

Diamond fairies are usually very clever. They learn new things quickly and have good memories. Diamond fairies like to find out how everything works and enjoy puzzles and quizzes. They often don't like getting up in the mornings!

The Fairy Fashion Show

There is a lot of excitement among the fairies.
There's a new fashion show coming to Fairyland!

Blossom visited the fashion fairies in their
secret underground burrow. They were
busily sewing outfits for the show.

Blossom kindly offered to help out.
To her delight, Rosebud, the fashion
fairy, said she could model some clothes!

There was plenty to do before the show! Bluebell braided Blossom's hair with flowers, and fixed her make-up.

Blossom felt very nervous as the music began and she stepped out onto the stage!

The fashion show was a great success! Blossom didn't put a foot wrong as she paraded in the fabulous clothes.

Blossom modelled the most beautiful dress of all. When the show ended she didn't want to take it off!

But Rosebud gave Blossom the dress as a 'thank you' present for all her help!

✳ Blossom and the Dragonfly ✳

It had been a morning of sunshine and showers. Now it was dry again Blossom, Nettle and Bluebell were playing outside. They were happily leap-frogging over red-spotted toadstools when the Fairy Queen passed by in her carriage.

"Fairies!" the Queen called out. "I've got a very special job for you to do. Because of the weather, we've had lots of rainbows today. I was hoping you could

Thank you, fairies!

collect the gold fairy dust from the ends of the rainbows." The Fairy Queen handed Blossom a big basket to collect the gold fairy dust in.

"See you later," she waved as her carriage headed off in the direction of the palace.

Blossom and her friends set off excitedly. Looking for the glittering gold fairy dust was a favourite task!

"Here's some!" Nettle shouted a little later. "Oooh, it's *sooo* pretty!"

"You're supposed to put the gold dust in the basket – not all over yourself!" Bluebell giggled.

Before long the basket was almost full, when they heard a cry.

"Help, help!"

"Stop singing so loudly, Nettle!" Blossom shushed. "I can hear someone in trouble."

The fairies found a large dragonfly trapped in a bramble bush.

"Don't wriggle," Bluebell told the dragonfly as she struggled to free it.

Will it hurt?

"Thank you," the dragonfly replied gratefully. "But oh dear, look at my poor torn wing. The brambles have completely ruined it."

The fairies stared at the broken wing in dismay.

"I know," said Bluebell. "I'm good at sewing. I'll weave a new wing using silken threads from a spider's web."

With Spidey's kind help Bluebell had soon finished stitching the wing.

"There! It doesn't look bad."

The dragonfly flapped his wing gently to try it out.

"It works perfectly," he said, darting here and there. "But it doesn't shimmer and glint in the light like my old wing did."

The fairies had to agree that the new wing looked a little dull. But no one could think of how to make it shimmery again.

"The Fairy Queen might have an idea," Blossom told the dragonfly brightly. "Why don't you come back to the palace with us?"

The dragonfly had never been inside the palace before. As the footman showed them in all the fairies curtsied and presented the Fairy Queen with the basket full of gold fairy dust.

Well done!

"Please, Your Majesty, here is your basket," said Blossom proudly. Then she explained what had happened to the dragonfly. The Fairy Queen laughed.

"You are holding what you need to help the poor dragonfly," she said with a smile. And she reached into the basket and took out a handful of the sparkly gold dust.

The moment she sprinkled it over the dragonfly's wing it shimmered and glinted – just as it should!

Thank you, fairy friends.

⋆ What Kind of Fairy are You? ⋆

If you lived in Fairyland,
what sort of fairy would you be?
Try our quiz and find out. On a piece
of paper, write each answer you
would choose.

1. The perfume fairies ask you to test their
new scent. It smells terrible! What do you do?
A) Be honest, then spend all day helping
them brew up a new mixture.
B) Hold your nose and pretend to faint!
C) Say you love it — you don't want
to hurt their feelings.

2. A small fairy asks to use your
new glitter make-up. Do you:
A) Say yes and ask if you can
borrow her sparkly hairclips.
B) Tell her no. You're fed up with
other fairies using your stuff.
C) Say yes and kindly offer to
show her how to wear it best.

3. You've been invited to the Fairy
May Ball and can't afford to buy
a new dress. What do you do?
A) Sew ribbons and sequins onto an old
dress and make it look as good as new.
B) Stay at home.
C) Go and enjoy yourself anyway —
it doesn't really matter what you wear.

4. Your best fairy friend tells you she's moving to another Fairyland on the other side of the world. Would you:

A) Look forward to receiving lots of interesting postcards from her.

B) Drop your friend immediately and start looking for a new best friend.

C) Give her a wonderful leaving party.

Oh, no! I've forgotten Jason's birthday!

5. It's your little elf brother's birthday and you've forgotten to buy him a present. Would you:

A) Pretend you're giving him a surprise later and rush out and buy something.

B) Find one of your old toys you don't want any more and quickly wrap it.

C) Give him the lovely big box of chocolates you'd been saving for yourself.

How did you score?

Mostly A
You are a fun-loving fairy and are enthusiastic about everything you do. You stay cheerful even when things go wrong. Your happy personality means you'll always have lots of fairy friends.

Mostly B
Oh dear! You can be a little bit of a thoughtless fairy sometimes. Try to be a bit more generous and join in more with all the other fairy activities and you'll have lots more fun!

Mostly C
You are everyone's favourite fairy friend. You are kind and considerate and always thinking of others. Give yourself a big pat on the back – the Fairy Queen would be proud of you!

✳ Autumn Nature-Spotting ✳

We're going nature-spotting in the countryside. We're hoping to see lots of exciting creatures! I'm taking some binoculars and, on the way, Nettle is going to teach us the Fairy Country Code.

Hmm, gnawed bark – must have been a squirrel.

Gosh, three fox cubs!

Wild animals are very shy and secretive. They'll often hide away when they see fairies coming. So, to spot them, the fairies will have to be very patient and quiet!

I see two mice!

Me too!

Nibbled seeds can mean that some mice or voles have been feeding close by. Lavender has spotted something in the grass.

Squeak!

Bluebell has found a fox's den under a tree. She is being as silent as she can as she watches excitedly to see if any baby foxes come out to play.

The Fairy Country Code
1. Keep to the fairy footpaths.
2. Take litter home with you.
3. Close gates behind you to stop farm animals escaping.
4. Don't pick any flowers or plants.
5. Do not disturb the animals.
6. Don't spoil the countryside for other fairies.

I've just come across this tuft of animal hair caught on a fence. I think it has come from a sheep.

Look, Blossom! A deer!

Look, Thumper! A fairy!

This time we're the ones being followed!

A good way of tracking animals is by looking out for their footprints in the earth. Here are some bird tracks – I wonder what they'll lead us to…

·57·

Butterfly Mobile

Caw! Would you make a bird mobile next, Blossom?

Use the beautiful Fairyland butterfly stickers to make a mobile just like this!

You will need: Two sticks from the garden or park (about 18cm long)
1m length of narrow ribbon * Cotton thread * Fairyland stickers

1. Tie one end of the ribbon to the middle of the longer stick. Then tie the shorter stick halfway along the ribbon. The loose end of ribbon is for hanging the mobile up.

2. Take the butterfly stickers and match them back-to-back, locking one end of the cotton thread in between each pair. Cut the cotton to about 15cm in length.

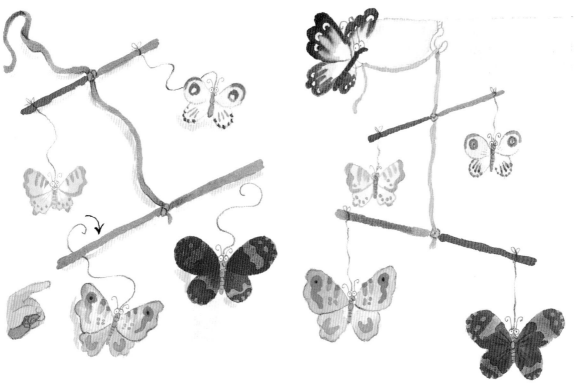

3. Tie the other end of each cotton thread to the sticks, as shown.

4. Ask an adult to tie your mobile up somewhere safely.

I've hung my mobile by the window.

They're shimmering, Blossom!

Look! There's one just like me!

Blossom Goes Camping

Blossom is excited. She and her friends are going camping in Fairyland woods. They've packed their rucksacks – let's hope they haven't forgotten anything important!

The fairies have walked deep into the woods. Hightail flies overhead to watch for danger.

Blossom and her friends are all sharing a big tent that they have made themselves.

There's such a lot to be done before nightfall.

Everything is unpacked and all the jobs are done. Supper is ready too!

It's getting dark now and the stars are twinkling overhead in the night sky.

After supper everyone sings the secret fairy camp song, to the tune of *'For He's a Jolly Good Fellow'*.

It's been a wonderful day, and now it's time for bed. No one feels the least bit sleepy, so Blossom tells one of her special bedtime stories. Turn the page to hear it too.

★ Snowdrop's Sale ★

$\mathcal{O}$nce upon a time, there was a fairy called Snowdrop. Snowdrop lived in a wood, on the far side of Fairyland. She loved her quiet house, which was in the hollow of a large apple tree. There was an empty tree house in the branches, and beneath the tree's roots was an old badger sett. In spring, this was smothered in bright yellow crocuses.

Snowdrop's home was rather big for one fairy – but Snowdrop thought it was just perfect. However, there was another problem. Very few fairies lived nearby. Poor Snowdrop sometimes got very lonely.

"If only I had some neighbours close by," Snowdrop sighed to herself one morning. "Perhaps I should move to a busier part of Fairyland."

The thought of leaving her apple tree standing empty was very sad, but she decided she must move. So she wrote out a huge 'For Sale' sign, and hung it from the branches of her apple tree. Then she set off towards the centre of Fairyland, to see if she could find herself somewhere new to live.

Snowdrop spent a busy morning flying around, searching for a suitable house. There was nothing she liked at all, so she decided to try again after lunch. But as she arrived back home, she had a surprise waiting for her. Sitting on her doorstep were two fairies.

"Hello," the fairies smiled at Snowdrop. "We were flying past when we spotted your 'For Sale' sign. We're looking for a new home and this apple tree looks lovely!"

Snowdrop was delighted. "Come inside and look around," she said, inviting them in.

The two fairies, called Posie and Rosie, were shown all over Snowdrop's tree hollow. When the tour had finished, they both looked a little embarrassed.

"We really only wanted to move into the empty tree house above," Rosie said.

"Yes,' added Posie. "We forgot to explain. It has a lovely view up there."

"Oh, sorry!" Snowdrop replied, feeling disappointed. "What a shame."

No sooner had Rosie and Posie waved goodbye, than there was another rat-a-tat-tat on the front door. Snowdrop answered it to find another smiling fairy.

"I'm Forget-me-not," said the fairy cheerily. "I noticed your 'For Sale' sign and rushed over. This place is just what I've been looking for!"

Happily, Snowdrop showed Forget-me-not all around her home.

"It's very nice," Forget-me-not said. "But I wanted to make my home in the empty badger sett. Badger setts are so cosy," she added.

Snowdrop was upset that no one seemed interested in her lovely home. She was feeling fed up with the whole idea of moving house already.

It was too late to go house-hunting that afternoon so Snowdrop baked some fairy cakes instead. She was just taking them out of the oven when another visitor arrived. This time it was a little fairy called Daisy, who had seen the sale sign.

"You do want a home in the tree's hollow?" Snowdrop checked with her. "Not in the branches or under the roots?"

Daisy assured Snowdrop she wanted a tree hollow, so Snowdrop invited her in. But although Daisy loved the house, she said it was far too big and lonely for her.

"It is large," Snowdrop agreed sadly, wondering if she would ever find someone who would like to live in her home. "The hollow is really meant for two fairies."

Then, all of a sudden, Snowdrop had a wonderful idea. "Wait here," she told Daisy. "Don't move! I'm off to find Rosie, Posie and Forget-me-not!"

Fortunately Snowdrop found them all looking at houses quite nearby. Together they returned to Daisy in the hollow, feeling quite puzzled.

"I only wanted to move so I could meet new friends," Snowdrop explained. "Now I've thought of a way I can have friends close by – without moving!"

Snowdrop's plan was that Rosie and Posie should move into the empty tree house, and Forget-me-not could live inside the old badger sett. Both houses had been empty for years and years.

"What about me?" piped up Daisy.

"The hollow is meant for two fairies," Snowdrop said excitedly. "Would you like to share the hollow with me? We could be great friends!"

A great cheer went up. It was the perfect solution.

"Now everyone's happy!" laughed Snowdrop, as she handed round a plateful of her delicious fairy cakes. She was so pleased. Not only could she stay in her lovely home – but she now had plenty of new friends around too!

✱ What Fairy Job would You Do? ✱

Would you prefer to work in Fairyland's perfume factory or become a fashion fairy? Do my quiz and find out what fairy job would most suit you. On a piece of paper, write down each answer you would choose.

1. It's a lovely sunny day. Would you most like to:
A) Meet your friends for a great picnic in Fairyland woods.
B) Go shopping and treat yourself to some new glittery jewellery.
C) Have fun taking the baby fairies swimming in the stream.

2. Your best friend asks you to help out at her little sister's birthday party. Do you:
A) Spend all day cooking up some delicious party treats.
B) Make lots of pretty brooches and rings for the young fairies to win as prizes.
C) Help with the party games, and make sure everyone's having fun.

3. You've just got home from a lovely holiday at the seaside. What's the first thing you do?
A) Just relax – it's great to be in your own home again.
B) Read the fab fashion magazine that arrived while you were away!
C) Rush round to see your friends.

4. You spot a fairy trail in the woods and decide to follow it. Where do you hope it leads to?
A) Your dream cottage in the middle of an apple orchard.
B) A treasure chest hidden deep in the forest.
C) A secret hide-out where your friends are waiting for you with a wonderful surprise!

5. You wake up to find Fairyland covered in deep snow. Do you:
A) Stay indoors – it looks freezing outside.
B) Dress up in your new snowsuit and go out sledging.
C) Organise a snowman-building competition!

How did you score?

Mostly A
You are a home-loving fairy and love cooking. You would enjoy working in the palace kitchens, or growing fruit and vegetables in the Fairy Queen's garden.

Mostly B
You love pretty trinkets and wearing the latest fairy fashions. A job making jewellery and gorgeous clothes with the fashion fairies would suit you perfectly.

Mostly C
You like being with fairies of all ages and love meeting new friends. You'd make a wonderful teacher at the Fairyland school, or you might enjoy a job as a post fairy.

Autumn and Winter Fashion Fun

It's getting cold again in Fairyland, and an exciting new fashion season has begun! My Boutique is full with all the latest fairy clothes and accessories.

I'm decorating my tiaras with jewels.

Caw!

Help, these boots are stuck!

Gift Wrapping Service

⋆ Glitter Snowstorm ⋆

I've chosen a jolly Father Christmas and reindeer toy for my snowstorm – it looks really Christmassy. You could use a pretty toy fairy!

You will need: A clear glass food jar, with a screw-on lid (choose a short, fat jar, with a nice lid) ⋆ White modelling clay ⋆ A plastic toy or Christmas novelty Glycerine (to slow the fall of the glitter) ⋆ Silver glitter ⋆ Blue food colouring

1. Wash the jar thoroughly and remove any labels. Make sure the jar is airtight.

Wheee!

2. Cover the inside of the lid with a mound of modelling clay to look like snow.

Your toy should be no bigger than the jar!

3. Push the toy or Christmas decoration firmly into the modelling clay and mould the clay around the toy to help keep it in place.

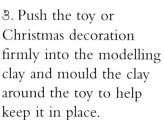

4. Check the instructions on the glycerine bottle and half fill your jar with glycerine. Top up with water until the jar is three-quarters full. Add a tablespoon of glitter and a few drops of the food colouring.

5. Carefully lower the lid onto the jar. The liquid will rise up.

6. If the liquid doesn't fill the jar completely, add a little more water. Then ask an adult to screw the lid on tightly.

Always use things that water won't spoil!

Wow!

So sparkly!

7. Give the jar a good shake and turn the jar the right way up. Watch the glitter fall like sparkling snow!

⋆ First Snow in Fairyland ⋆

One morning the fairies woke to find Fairyland covered in deep snow. Winter had arrived!

Blossom and her friends dressed warmly, and met up at the old oak tree. They had an important job to do – and quickly!

The fairies like to check that the animals and birds are ready for the winter. Snow causes all sorts of problems for the fairies' animal friends. First, the fairies headed for the palace.

Blossom and Lavender piled their sleigh high with food from the royal kitchens.

Meanwhile Bluebell and the others collected bags of thistledown bedding.

Once loaded up, everyone set off for Fairyland woods. It looked beautiful in the snow!

Three hungry squirrels raced out to meet the fairies. Blossom gave them some acorns.

Meanwhile, Nettle was checking that all the dormice were safely asleep in their nests.

One dormouse wasn't ready at all! Nettle's woolly hat made it a perfect instant nest!

Yawn!

That's better.

At Fairyland lake, the ducks were starving! They ate up all of the bread!

Quack!

Wheee!

Brrr, it's cold!

This will keep the wind out.

They looked inside the rabbit warrens. Many of them needed extra warm bedding.

Oh dear! One of the rabbit holes looked very draughty!

My mittens make great bird feeders!

Snug!

You'll be warm now.

The birds *were* pleased! They fluttered down to eat the seeds and nuts.

Finally, all the creatures had been taken care of. Happily, the fairies headed back through the snow.

There was a brilliant surprise waiting back home! Someone had left a pile of presents under the fairies' tree.

They were great 'thank you' gifts from the woodland creatures – and were exactly what everyone needed! Now no one will go cold this winter!